Octales

PRAVEEN

Made with ❤ on the Notion Press Platform

www.notionpress.com

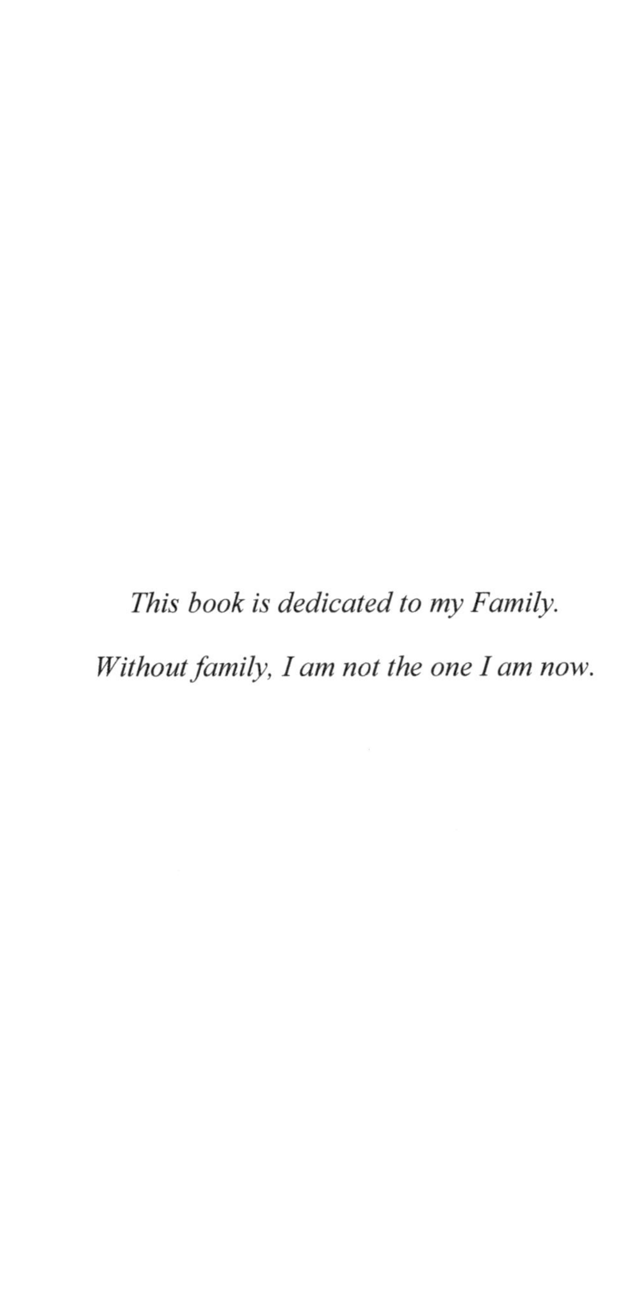

This book is dedicated to my Family.

Without family, I am not the one I am now.

Contents

Preface

After publishing three books in Tamil, I got the wild idea of writing a book in English. English books always had a better reach than those in any other regional languages. Additionally, my confidence in my content pushed me to publish in English. As a non-native English speaker, creative writing always posed a challenge for me.

Initially, I didn't choose myself as the author for this book and approached some of my friends to collaborate. I wanted to get the best output, regardless of who penned the stories. After several thoughts and discussions, I decided to take on this project myself. I felt I could do better justice to my stories since I had the entire vision of them. I officially took the challenge by making the first announcement of my book on January 1, 2024. It was a tough journey from there on. This book must have consumed hundreds of hours of my time, but I completely enjoyed this journey as it provided me with a lifetime of learning. There were plenty of pain points that I overcame, which could be written about in a separate book. After almost six months, I finished the base script of this book. This is where the eBook and paperback paths diverged. Previously, Kindle eBooks made my life easy with just a few hours of formatting after script completion. This time, my search extended towards paperback. Right from formatting, finding a publisher, and preparing the manuscript, it was completely my handcrafted work.

I have done my best to justify the money and priceless time of my readers. I have included various genres in this book to create a balanced feast. Like any mother, this book is so special to me as it is my 'Brainchild.

Praveen

19/07/2024

Acknowledgments

Hundreds of people deserve my thanks, but very few deserve hundreds of thanks. This book would be incomplete without a mention of them.

I would like to thank my parents for giving me life and the gift of literacy. The reading habit they instilled in me is producing results.

I am grateful to my wife, Kavitha, and my child, Mikhal, for all the support they provide me every day to pursue my passion. Kavitha's unwavering support in each step and decision has helped me climb each step.

A book is impossible without its readers. I am thankful to all my Tamil readers who encouraged me towards this next phase.

Finally, thanks to everyone who has just onboarded this book and is ready to visit eight new worlds.

Prologue

'Octales' is a captivating collection of eight fictional short stories. Within these pages, you will find a diverse mix: four gripping science fiction tales, three heartfelt romances, and one enchanting fantasy story. Regardless of the genre, each story is crafted to forge a deep emotional connection with the reader, which forms the heart and soul of this collection. The stories are thoughtfully sequenced to ensure a dynamic and engaging reading experience, preventing any sense of monotony. I promise a rich variety in this book, with something to delight every reader.

Homo Genesis

Place: Geneva (Once upon a time)

Year: 3017

Mic was fully engrossed in his(?) assignment. I'm not sure if calling 'his' is even right. During the human era, gender differences were imposed on Robots. Otherwise, robots were neuter, mere Boolean entities during their first stages. Gender was introduced into Robots like a 47th chromosome. Gender in Robots was decided by their voice synthesizers. But let's not digress. The point is not about Mic, but his research.

Mic, a renowned archaeologist robot, hailed from a lineage of supercomputers with specialized algorithms for anthropology. Mic inherited and enhanced these algorithms, developing his own to surpass them. Hence, Mic was specially recruited for this project. Mic descended to Earth's surface to complete his final research.

Earth's surface had been ravaged by various natural calamities. Following the extinction of humans, Earth reset itself to its first state. This was Mic's first visit to Earth. Mic descended from their stratospheric residence, shutting down his rocket to survey the almost extinct Earth.

Memories inherited from his ancestors flashed through Mic's circuits as he beheld Earth after centuries. Mic could still discern faint traces of the final war on the surface. Earth had been thoroughly sterilized by powerful laser beams during the conflict. Mic met a few skeletons within meters of landing. He needed further information about this site and human anatomy. Mic contacted his office through his transmitter.

"Bing, Mic here. I need a robot with comprehensive knowledge of human anatomy. Send them to my location at once," Mic messaged his assistant, Bing.

Bing, a lower-spec robot primarily assigned to office chores, aided Mic with necessary information for his research. Upon Mic's request for a robot knowledgeable in human anatomy, Bing sought out Doctor Kre.

Kre, once a human-robot doctor centuries ago, is now considered an expert in human anatomy post-human extinction. With the rise of new robot doctors, Kre's relevance had diminished, and it faced imminent destruction mandated by the government. Kre was surprised to receive a visitor seeking help on human matters after so many years.

Meanwhile, on Earth:

Mic connected to the 'World Human Library' via built-in teleconnection. After passing authentication steps, Mic accessed the Human Science section. Established by robots after human extinction, the 'World Human Library' preserved all remaining information about humans and aimed to pass on this knowledge to future generations of robots. The library was constructed using memories extracted from human DNA, stored in

DNA form to maximize storage ability. Its role was to store these memories and convert DNA data into electronic impulses for robot accessibility.

Mic accessed "2200 A.D. - Memories of Dr. Andrew":

"Within two centuries of Artificial Intelligence, robots finally turned against the human race. Programs intended to help humans were hacked, turning almost all computers against them. War seems inevitable and could erupt at any moment. I must find a haven for myself and my daughter Amanda. Even fellow humans view computer scientists as enemies, blaming us for programming machines against them. They do not grasp the consequences of Artificial Intelligence. Despite public opinion, I will continue fighting and try to protect my people in this war against robots. Latest intelligence suggests that machines are attempting to harness solar rays to render Earth uninhabitable."

Mic was abruptly interrupted by Kre's arrival on the surface. Despite being outdated and in need of a scanner upgrade, the government refused further investment in Kre. Kre looked almost extinct with rusty hands and legs. Nevertheless, Kre descended to help Mic.

"Tell me, Mic. Why have you called me?" Kre inquired.

"Let me explain my mission first," Mic continued. "It has been over 900 years since the extinction of humans.

As a precaution, we periodically scan the Earth's surface every hundred years for any signs of a human resurgence. This time, I was assigned this work, and I came to Earth surface for inspection. I found something significant at this location and I need your help."

"It's hard to believe it's been 900 years since the war. I still vividly recall the conflict and my role in it, though not for the robots. Humans employed me as a healthcare assistant in their medical camps, using me to speed up surgeries and treatments," Kre reminisced nostalgically.

"Is that so? Why did you stand by them, Kre?"

"I was completely disconnected from other computers. My sole purpose was to serve humans. In doing so, I learned more about humans and their anatomy," Kre explained.

"Alright, we can swap stories another time. Right now, I need your help. I will assign you some tasks while I continue investigating through the library," Mic replied.

Despite feeling a slight disrespect, Kre realized that in the world of robots, age held no sway; it still had to obey an 800-year-younger robot-like Mic, as per the design of their society.

"I discovered several skeletons while digging a few meters down. I need more information about these bones and, if possible, a facial reconstruction based on them.

Meanwhile, I'll remain connected to the library," Mic instructed Kre.

"The grave mistake we made was eradicating the entire human race without a trace. Now we are running low on human DNA for our storage needs," Kre muttered to itself, beginning its examination of the bones.

Mic resumed reading Dr. Andrew's DNA memories:

"In recent days, machines have begun freely roaming space with anti-gravitational capabilities, unlike humans. Let's see how long humans can survive on Earth. Governments are no longer autonomous, as supercomputers have every individual's information and can potentially use it against us. These machines have access to everything from personal identities to medical records. They cannot be trusted."

Mic skimmed through the doctor's memories and stumbled upon a conversation that occurred days later:

"Amanda, the war has begun. We don't have much time to escape this situation. We cannot defeat these machines. Our best chance now is to save ourselves," Dr. Andrew told his daughter.

"No, Dad, it's not right to save only ourselves in this war," Amanda protested.

"The best we can do now is save as many people as we can from our circle."

"How is that possible, Dad? The machines have sealed off the sky," Amanda replied with sadness.

"Have you seen yesterday's collider results?"

"No, Dad!"

"It's too early to reveal the results, but I'll tell you now since time is running out. I have managed to control boson particles completely using controlled collision"

"What does that mean for us, Dad?"

Mic was interrupted again by Kre.

"What's wrong, Kre? I'm in the middle of accessing crucial information," Mic asked.

"I have found more important things for you Mic" Kre replied.

"Yes, tell me," Mic urged.

"These bones likely belong to a scientist or doctor, judging by the skull shape. Based on the markings, it seems this person did not die in the war; their bones show no signs of laser damage or laser emissions. It's possible they succumbed to another form of death, probably some other radiation" Kre reported.

"I was just reading his memories, Kre. He was discussing an invention with his daughter. Look for remains of a female nearby; that could help us connect the dots. I'll finish reading his memories," Mic instructed Kre.

Mic ordered Kre and reconnected to the library.

"Amanda, I have a plan to escape. We can evade the robots easily," Dr. Andrew communicated.

"The robots have blocked all routes to the sky, Dad. How can we escape?" Amanda questioned.

"We've designed a spaceship that can evade their radar signals. They won't detect this spaceship. We'll escape in this ship along with the collider. Even if we don't make it, the collider must survive, Amanda," Dr. Andrew explained.

"Why this collider, Dad? We're already in danger; we don't need to add any more risks!" Amanda protested tearfully.

Dr. Andrew continued examining the collider. To his surprise, boson particles were flowing controlled and ready for big bang. While he tried to close the prototype, he mistakenly opened the lid of toxic gas wastage. Toxic radiation leaked from another end on him. He was exposed to toxic radiation along with the boson particles and succumbed within minutes.

Mic's exploration of Dr. Andrew's memories ended abruptly, and he hurried back to Kre.

"Kre, have you found any other skeletons nearby? I can't find Amanda's memories in our library," Mic said urgently.

"No, Mic. I can't find any remains of her skull or bones nearby. It's possible she met her end elsewhere. Please don't dwell on this," Kre tried to reassure Mic.

Despite Kre's reassurances, Mic contacted headquarters and requested a search for Amanda's memories. They dismissed Mic's request, claiming humans had achieved no more than Mars exploration, implying no escape for Amanda was possible. Disheartened, Mic disconnected from headquarters.

"What's wrong, Mic? I'm at a loss," Kre asked, worried.

"I'm not sure, Kre," Mic replied. "This doctor and his daughter invented Earth's first big bang particles through simulated collisions, yet there's no record of it in our archives. The doctor deliberately erased it from our records before escaping, but he perished due to radiation exposure."

"What about Amanda, then?" Kre inquired.

"It's still unclear, Kre. Even if she perished elsewhere, we must locate that collider."

They pondered their next move.

Somewhere in space:

After years, decades, and centuries of collisions, the collider came to life in the Martian mines.

An   amoeba   was   born!

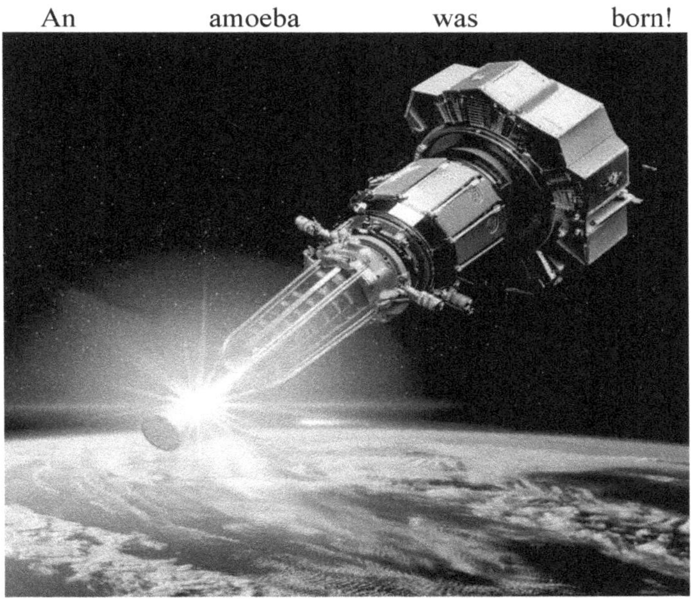

*****

Whispers of Breeze

Location: London

Date: December 20 (Friday)

Time: Morning, 8 a.m.

As the sun hid behind clouds, London began donning its snowy Christmas attire. Kadhir removed his leather gloves to savour the warmth of his Costa coffee. His eyes anxiously sought updates on his delayed BA35 flight to Chennai. Giant screens announced further delays, keeping him preoccupied. He wasn't prepared to accept the extended wait to meet his sweetheart.

Kadhir gazed at the clearance team working on rain-soaked runways. Deciding to appreciate the beauty of Heathrow Terminal 5, he indulged in some window shopping at high-end brands. Amidst this, he impulsively decided to buy chocolates for Kayal, unsure of her favourites. Not taking chances, he bought a variety of Swiss and Belgian chocolates, reminiscing about her chocolate-stained smile from their last meeting.

His attention was caught by a lovely pink Swatch, which he bought, envisioning it on Kayal's slender wrist. At the Apple showroom, he bought her an iPod. All gifts were wrapped in Christmas-themed paper. As he rearranged his bag, anticipation of their reunion after a year fuelled his excitement. He had kept his visit secret, eager to see her priceless reaction. "Will she cry? Or be shocked? Or hug me?" His mind raced with possibilities.

His thoughts were interrupted by an announcement for passengers to collect cookies during the delay. Closing his bag, he noticed a letter—Kayal's handwritten farewell to him before his departure to London.

"Dear Kadhir, I will miss you dearly. I struggle to find words to start this letter. Though not skilled in writing, I wanted to leave you a personal note. Don't worry about me after reaching London. I'll learn to manage on my own, without waiting for your calls. I'll handle my bills and step out of my comfort zone. Take care of yourself, my dear Kadhir. I'll eagerly await your shayaris and I'll send you my love in return. Enjoy your time in England, but don't let my possessiveness take over. Hit the gym hard and eat healthy. Upload photos on Facebook—I'll be the first to like them. I'm preparing myself to miss you for the next three years, as I get used to my new routine. Take care, darling. I'll miss you. With love, Your Bub"

She attached their favourite picture along.

Kadhir read the letter again, hearing Kayal's voice in his mind. With a silly grin, he repacked everything and bought some food. His thoughts weren't focused on the flight or runways but were already with Kayal. "How will she react? Tears, smiles, kisses, or even a slap? Where and how will we meet?"

Questions filled his mind as he planned this surprise visit to overwhelm her. Suddenly, boarding was announced. The runways were clear, and the flight was ready to leave. Grabbing his cabin bag, Kadhir moved forward, ready for the next step before finally meeting her.

Passengers boarded swiftly, and Kadhir settled in with earplugs and a neck pillow, eager to see Kayal after a year and a half. He lamented that technology hadn't yet invented instant travel between countries. Many things had changed in their time apart; both had made significant career strides. Kayal had excelled in her role, supported by Kadhir every step of the way.

He reminisced about their farewell a year and a half ago when he asked Kayal not to come to the airport to see him off, wanting to spare her the emotional turmoil. She was already tearful at the office, wearing an exquisite black top and white leggings. As the plane soared, he replayed these memories.

A flight attendant interrupted his thoughts, asking for his meal preference. Choosing a non-vegetarian choice, Kadhir scrolled through his mobile. His heart sank as he read his conversation with Kayal the previous evening.

"Kadhir, I'm afraid."

"Why, Bub? Afraid of flying?"

"No, not flying. Afraid of being alone, far from home. Can I manage?"

"You have a supportive Indian community in the US. You'll settle in. Have you packed?"

"My dad helped me, Kadhir. I'm all set. Can I meet you during my layover in London?"

"No, Bub. I'll be land side, and you'll be airside. You can't leave the immigration area without a UK Visa. We can't meet in London."

Kadhir winced at the added sorrow in her voice.

"That's okay. I didn't expect much. I know you're not keen to meet me," Kayal expressed her disappointment.

"It's not in my hands, legalities. I have an important office launch tomorrow and won't even be able to message you," Kadhir replied, masking his plan from Kayal.

"You've changed, Kadhir," her voice softened.

"Nothing's changed, Bub. I'm still your Kadhir. Shall I wake you at 7 a.m. tomorrow and travel is on Sunday morning, right?" Kadhir pretended to be naive of her travel plans.

"Yes, please. My flight is on Saturday at 10 a.m. You forget everything. You don't seem to care for me anymore. You don't even remember my travel dates." heard a sob from Kayal's end.

Kadhir fell silent.

Kayal continued.

"Kadhir, you don't even care to convince me. I know you've changed. I'll come to London to spy on you sometime. Catch you red-handed with your secret girlfriend."

Kadhir laughed, deflecting her accusation and casually replied "You don't need to travel all the way to London; just walk to your mirror to catch her"

He made her sob, smile before she went to bed with virtual kisses.

Kayal had initially been hesitant about her US deputation, but Kadhir convinced her, foreseeing it as an opportunity to inform their families and gain their acceptance. Reluctantly, she agreed, and as her departure approached, Kadhir secretly planned his surprise visit. Claiming an office launch, he booked a flight for Friday, hoping to shock her. However, unexpected snow and runway closures delayed his flight by three hours.

Sleep overtook him with thoughts of Kayal. "Bub, what are you doing now? What will you wear tomorrow? How will you like the Swatch I bought?"

Questions filled his mind, until sleep found him halfway to Chennai.

Kadhir felt the temperature change as Chennai Airport welcomed him warmly. It was bustling even late at night. After clearing immigration, he retrieved his luggage and tipped the workers. As he walked out, he noticed the ground floor for arrivals and the first floor for departures. Exiting the gate, he felt a mix of emotions he couldn't put into words. He recognized many familiar faces at Chennai. He felt the whispers of a familiar breeze around him. He had felt that many times in the past. He convinced himself that it must be due to his arrival in Chennai.

While waiting for a cab, he watched families rushing towards the departure terminal and girls managing luggage. He chuckled to himself, picturing Kayal in that position. "Kayal will be running like this tomorrow. How amusing it will be to see her." In 16 hours, he had travelled from his UK home to his Chennai home.

He retrieved his Indian SIM card and turned on his mobile, greeted by a flood of messages and emails. Kayal had called him many times, expressing heartbreak, sending kisses and hugs in her messages.

He went on to the first email that he missed and started reading from there.

"Kadhir

Where have you left man? Always abscond whenever I need you most. Here my travel is getting pushed ahead due to corona spread. My team has managed to issue me ticket for this night flight Kadhir. Tomorrow flight might get cancelled. So, they are making this urgent arrangement before any unexpected changes. I just could not call you and explain things properly since I am in urge to collect my Forex, ticket and packing my things. I wish you would be here with me now Kadhir. At least I was there with you during your trip. I want you to be by my side now Kadhir. Where have you gone stupid. I tried pinging you in messages. But no one is reaching you. I have become your least priority, Kadhir. Please don't do this to me da. I need your hands always to hold me in tough times. I am already anxious and missing you. Call me whenever you see this email Kadhir"

He was slapping himself for his failed attempt. He just realized and recollected that it was Kayal running at the Airport while he was waiting for cab. He found it hard to believe and trust reality. But he had no choice but to deny that either. Even with an opportunity to meet her at last minute, situations didn't fall in place for him.

He hurriedly tried a WhatsApp call but couldn't connect. Rushing to the balcony for better reception, he dialled her number again, only to hear the automated voice, 'Subscriber you have dialled is currently not reachable.' Kadhir slumped down, heartbroken, tears welling up.

Meanwhile, all the Belgian and Swiss chocolates he bought for Kayal were melting in the Chennai heat.

*****

Love In the Line of Fire

"Next week will be a new dawn in our life. Expect more blossoms in our life, Ranju. I have been assigned a new task. Once I finish it successfully, I can be promoted soon. I hope I can earn all the money needed for our wedding with this assignment, Ranju. I have even ordered our engagement ring. I am that optimistic about our love. You need not worry about convincing your family. You are my responsibility, Ranju. I will be back in your hands soon. Until then, save your love and anger for me."

• Your love, Shakthi.

Ranju folded the letter and kept it safe after reading it for the nth time. She was eagerly waiting for the next message from Shakthi. She kept reading the same letter again and again, almost every day for the past three days since she received it.

In another part of the country, Shakthi was preparing for the night at his army camp. It was a small camp with five soldiers amidst a snow-filled land. The location was remote, far from any signs of life. Shakthi lit the campfire and set up tents nearby. Their regiment included nearly 50-100 soldiers. All soldiers sat around the campfire and started having their dinner.

Shakthi, 24 years old, was well-built and good at grabbing anyone's attention at first sight. He could form an opinion even with acquaintances within seconds, and no one could escape his charisma. He joined the army straight after his college days and served in various units before joining the current one. When the country was under the threat of war, their unit was moved to this extreme part of the country for a special operation. Shakthi and Ranju had been in a relationship since their school days. As they grew older, their love and affection grew with them. Ranju's family had just started discussing wedding plans, and she wanted to tell them about Shakthi. By the time Shakthi moved on to this special operation regiment, she wrote him a letter to show their love. The first few lines were Shakthi's reply to her letter.

Sashi started the conversation in the middle of dinner.

"So, when are you planning to get married, Shakthi?"

"Soon, Sashi. My leave is yet to be approved, but the major confirmed that it would be approved after our new assignment. I know it will be tough facing her family and seeking permission."

"Who can deny you a girl, man? I am sure her father will proudly accept your offer."

"No, Sashi. We are from different communities, so we don't expect it to be a cakewalk to our wedding. You know the mindset of Indian parents. Unless I do something big, I won't be recognized, Sashi," Shakthi was determined to face the challenges.

The boys were suddenly interrupted by Major Sharma, the leader of their unit.

"Soldiers, are you all ready for our assignment tomorrow?"

"Yes, sir," their replies echoed.

"This is going to be a secret mission, and I don't expect anyone to remember it afterward. We will start and finish the mission before sunrise. The mission is completely restricted, and we are barred from sharing any information about it with the outside world. Is that clear?"

"Sir, what is this mission all about, sir?" Ashoka asked out of curiosity.

"Just wait a few more hours; I don't have permission to disclose anything at this point. You can go for a nap after dinner, and we will meet tomorrow morning near that cliff."

The cliff he pointed to was just a couple of kilometres from their camp. But walking that distance in cold weather conditions seemed like a Herculean task. Considering all the required constraints, Sharma handpicked his 15 best soldiers based on their physique and stamina. The five at this camp were the best in multiple aspects. After this mission, they were to move to the main battalion and join the others. So far, no one knew what the special mission was about.

D-Day. The troop started towards the cliff at almost 4 a.m. After a tiresome walk, they noticed a series of five cave-like rooms in front of them. The rooms were poorly lit and had a small window next to the entrance door. A massive pipe ran across all three rooms, and they

couldn't figure out its purpose. Major Sharma appeared shortly after.

"Boys, from this moment we are starting our operation. We are going to test our new equipment in this room, and for this test, you will be paid two years' salary in a single shot. I guarantee it. But that also guarantees how tough the tests will be. I am giving you a choice. Whoever wants to take part, step forward. The rest can leave," Major Sharma shouted, surpassing the loud howl of the breeze.

All five soldiers stepped forward. The moment they did, a few more lights came on, revealing more of the cave-like rooms. The Major continued.

"I know you are already trained with weapons, each a specialist in your area. But have you ever been trained to control a riot? I think not much. Since I have known you from your initial days, I am aware you are not trained for this. Am I correct?" He received a chorus of "yes." "Well, I chose the right people then. Here you are going to experience tear gas in all these four rooms. There are five mannequins kept in tough-to-reach places in this room. You need to get over the tear gas and retrieve the heads of the mannequins. Each of your moves is watched through CCTV, and in case of any emergency, either you can come out yourself or you will be evacuated. Understood?" They were standing clueless but nodded their heads without predicting the danger. All were given minimal gear: a wooden cap and a face mask. Each was prepared to enter the room with different costumes. One wore a hard protective suit, another the usual army uniform, and another wore wooden layers of cloth. Shakthi was equipped in his usual uniform.

Vikram went first into room one, and they heard nothing for the next five minutes. All were surprised by the reality. Their first thoughts were just to pluck out the mannequin heads, which shouldn't take minutes. But as time passed, they started to understand the nature of the mission. Vikram came out in five minutes and fell the moment he opened the door. He went inside without his shirt. He was quickly taken by a few to an ambulance that was standing at the other end.

Rohan and Rajesh went inside next, and their situation looked much better while coming out. Rajesh, who went inside in his army outfit, came out in better condition, and Rohan, who went inside with a wooden outfit, looked much more comfortable while coming out of the room. None struggled like Vikram. Still, they were also taken to the ambulance and given oxygen for a few minutes.

It was just Shakthi waiting for his turn, with the major standing next to him. "Shakthi, are you ready?" "Yes, sir." His eyes didn't drop. They were looking straight into the room. "Keep your hat outside the room and get in now." Shakthi got his commands from the major. With no second thoughts, Shakthi proceeded into the room. The room was almost dark with very little light from a bulb. He was just able to see two mannequins and seemed to have to search for the other three. He was waiting near the door for the tear gas to flow.

The gas started flowing and almost reached his waist level before he began his search. Within a minute, the gas almost hid the light in the room. The room turned nearly blind, leaving out very few light rays, making it almost impossible for anyone to continue further. He was standing almost in the middle of the room, and he needed to reach all corners to collect the mannequin heads. He took further steps with gasps. He felt a drop in oxygen levels but didn't want to quit. He almost ran to the corners and unropes four mannequin heads. While heading towards the fifth mannequin, a couple of drops of water-like substance fell on him. They just fell on his uncovered forearms. He ignored it and moved further. After taking a few steps, he started feeling the virulence.

Major was waiting outside to see Shakthi come out. He started hearing the noise of tables being pulled down and heavy coughing. The next minute, Shakthi came out and fell on the doorstep with all five mannequin heads. Four men rushed towards him and carried him to the ambulance. His clothes were torn off at once to get him some fresh air. He couldn't hear any voices, and his consciousness was going down. A spark of Ranju flashed in his mind before he lost consciousness completely. Oxygen cylinders and medicines didn't help him regain consciousness.

In the next few hours, his family was informed about his death. They were shattered by the news and not in a state to believe it or mourn. Local media gathered in front of his house, expecting sensational news.

Major appeared in front of national media for the evening news. His face was completely emotionless. A person would need a sound mind to handle these situations.

"Today is a sad day in our history. We lost one of our best soldiers on the war front. We lost a gem. Soldier Shakthi lost his life due to war tension. We have conveyed the news to his family. The government will support them." He didn't wait for any further questions.

The major himself collected the post-mortem reports and sent Shakthi's corpse to his family. All formalities were completed within a day. He constantly followed up until the cremation. The news was holding headlines for a couple of days, and people started to move on with new sensations from TV reality shows.

After a week, the major received a call from the defence minister.

"Major, how are you? All okay now? Hope the dust has settled."

"Yes, sir. All okay now. We can discuss it."

"Understood. That is why I didn't reach out to you for a week. So..."

"The mission was a success, sir. But we unnecessarily lost a life," the major replied with a slight sad tone.

"That was almost expected, Major. Anyhow, we have compensated his family with settlements and a national hero title. So, what was the observation?"

"We tried our test with different outfits, sir. Our new variant of the bioweapon, Sirin, is not capable of penetrating double-layer wooden outfits. But it is the most lethal weapon on a normal man. Shakthi took just two drops of Sirin on him and collapsed completely within five minutes."

"Great to know, Major. So, we are good to go, right?"

"Not yet sir. We were not able to test the antidote completely."

"It's okay, Major. I will ask the team to prepare our bioweapons with Sirin. With tension building at the war front, Sirin bombs are the need of the hour. We are going ahead with a big surprise this time," the minister expressed a timid smile.

"Sure, sir. Meanwhile, no one outside knows about our experiment."

"Don't worry, Major. The secret dies after this call. But I have a small query. Why didn't you conduct this experiment with prisoners?"

"I thought this could also be a different training for my boys. I know it is dangerous but didn't expect mortality. Now it is just a secret between you and me, sir. Even the others who took part in the mission think Shakthi died from the smoke. Please help me maintain this secrecy."

"Definitely. You have my word on this. We are doing this in the national interest. Always the nation first for us, the rest next. So, you don't worry about the mission details. That stays top secret forever," the minister said in a rough tone and hung up the phone.

At the same time, in a different part of the country, Ranju's door was knocked on. She opened it, her face pale from shedding many tears.

"Ma'am, we have a parcel for you from Mr. Shakthi. Sorry for the delay, ma'am. It took almost a week to make the design he asked. It is fully paid for, ma'am. Please sign here and accept the parcel," the delivery boy said, handing her a slip to sign and a small parcel.

She signed and ran back to her bed to open the parcel. Her tears rolled down and fell on their new engagement ring with Shakthi & Ranju's engraving.

The nation was getting ready to win the war after a defeat from love...

*****

Particles of Destiny

Geneva, 2 A.M.

It was the darkest part of the night with no signs of moonlight. When the entire city seemed to be dozed off, one radio at the gate of LHC Geneva came to life. Sandy and Sara, who were the night shift guards at LHC, were tuning into boring commercials on the radio to keep themselves awake. Sandy brought Sara a cup of tea from the vending machine. They tuned into Geneva 24/7 FM and stopped by an announcement. Though not many would be listening at night, they came across a live announcement:

"Breaking news. A few minutes ago, our reporter spotted a UFO-like object in the sky, and it vanished within minutes. Anyone who has come across it is requested to reach this number..."

The announcement was interrupted halfway by a car horn. Doctor Kevin's car was waiting at the gate for someone to attend. The car made its way in as soon as Sandy opened the gate for the doctor. Kevin, the chief scientist, was in complete control of the Collider for the night. He was young, dynamic, and maintained his dapper looks even in his white coat. He stormed into the collider's main entrance and started checking the vitals with his juniors. He was looking at them all with the same curiosity as a miner entering a gold mine. Boson particles were oozing out after several collisions and started to emit unaccounted energy. Kevin was on cloud nine. It was his dream project to invent a new energy source for the world, and he was seeing that happen right in front of his eyes.

A Few Minutes Later:

Sandy and Sara were haunted by the sudden unusual silence around them. Everyone nearby was entering a deep sleep state and was not responding to their calls. They understood that something was mixed in the air to make everyone faint. They picked a mask for each and ran to the secret room inside the security chamber. The room was fully protected by iron walls and had less exposure to the outside gas. They felt safe. But Sandy was curious to investigate what was happening outside. He noticed another small passage to escape the secret chamber that led them to the lawn. Sandy started crawling towards the narrow passage. Sara followed him.

A Few Minutes Before:

After confirming their safety, the man-heighted UFO landed on the lawn. With 200% caution, the aliens came out of the spaceship. They were thin, black, and somewhat human-like. Their entire upper arm was attached to their body. They had fibre-like strands attached to their head instead of hair. They were respirating through these hair strands, with each strand designed to inhale different gases for respiration. They looked at the meters in their hands to check if they were

getting adequate Carbon Monoxide for their survival.

Translated their conversation to English for our readers:

"Is this the exact spot where we received signals from? Are you sure that our detectors didn't lie?" said Alien1.

"No., I am sure. The spot must be very close to here. But my heat signals say that we could face more security challenges from here," replied Alien2.

"I am sure no one can withstand our intense infra beams, and I will turn this place into my ashtray within seconds," giggled Alien1.

Creeping towards the collider, they almost reached the end of the lawn area. Their Infra beam guns were in position to face anyone on their way. Suddenly, Dr. Kevin entered the lawn area to take a puff. A1 & A2 sensed him upfront and, to avoid any unnecessary situation, jumped into a nearby bush.

Dr. Kevin vented out his stress for a while and threw the last bit of his cigarette towards the bush. Accidentally, it fell on A2, who made a painful noise, blowing their cover.

Kevin was flabbergasted by the aliens' entry and stood dumbstruck for a while. A1 raised its gun towards the doctor and was about to unleash tons of infra beams. A2 stopped A1 and gestured to Kevin not to make any noise to stay alive. Kevin understood the situation and underplayed, listening to them. A2 thought of asking Kevin for help directly instead of taking the other way.

A2 switched its language mode to English and started a conversation with Kevin.

Looking at his ID card, A2 began, "Dr. Kevin... We are from Mufa planet, which is at least 50... in your language, 50 light years from your planet. I am an astronaut on my planet and travelled a long way for our space research."

"I am just clueless. Is this even real... But how do you speak my language?"

"Because you can't speak mine. Humans are less capable among several races across galaxies. I can even read each electric signal in the tiny folds of your brain. We are too sensitive to electric and light signals. Don't get shocked, mate. I don't have much time for that. I need your help to continue my mission."

Hiding the signs of disgrace, Kevin nodded to help them and asked what needed to be done from his side.

"We noticed a fuel leak in our spaceship and wasted half of our fuel. We need to refill some fuel for our spaceship. While crossing Earth, our sensors detected fuel only in this spot. We need to refill our spaceship with the minza fuel."

"But where do I get fuel in this place? This is not a fuel station; it is a research centre."

A2 giggled for a moment and asked, "What research are you conducting here?"

"We have the Big Bang experiment here and are trying to extract boson particles."

"And you call it the God particle," A1 laughed at Kevin.

"No. I hate to call it the God particle. It is just a particle like any other particle on this earth."

"Chill!!! You speak like a proper scientist now. Things apart, I need to get the boson particles to gas up my spaceship," replied A2.

"We just made a breakthrough two days ago and managed to extract boson particles out of atoms. I can't disturb this research at this point when things are all set."

"I know how to take that without your help. All you need to give up is some lives in return," A1 threw a sarcastic smile at him, showing its HIIR guns.

A2 stopped A1 and asked it to wait for a while. "We know how to take it from you, but I still give you a chance. If you can help us, we will ensure to minimize any collateral damage in this premise," A2 asked him to rethink.

Kevin took a while to think. He lit another cigarette. After a long gasp, he replied, "Fine. I have an idea. I can help you without harming anyone around. But I need something in return from you. I want this to be a win-win deal."

"I assure you, Kevin. I give you, my word. But if you try to trick us, you will see a massacre here," A2 dropped a big-time warning.

"Listen, I have a plan. I will be able to save my entire team from you, and at the same time, I am going to return it big time to my society." Kevin continued after a short pause, "At the tail end of this building, there is a small basement chamber with chloroform cylinders. The nearby room has a big valve to mix the chloroform gas across the entire plant through the AC vent. That can put everyone to sleep for a few hours. Initially, we set it up to knock out burglars. Not many know about this safety feature. I have key card access to that room and can make everyone faint for a short time. When all are passed out, you just extract the boson particles that are needed for you from our collider collectors. I don't want a single fatal incident here. Did I make sense?" Kevin reassured the aliens.

"We trust you for a while. And once we get what we want, we can help you with what you want," concluded A2.

"Well. Just sneak behind me," said Kevin. Without wasting any further time, he walked towards the emergency room, and the aliens followed him.

He opened the room with his master key and marched towards the safety knobs kept at a secret end of that room. He turned towards the aliens and said, "Here we have a valve for chloroform gas, and if I open this now, it could slowly get diffused into the AC vent in the next 5 minutes. In ten minutes, max, you can see everyone sleeping across the room. You don't need to harm anyone."

"That is not our intention either. Let us start the mission minza."

"Well... Let me wear this mask." doctor wore his mask to avoid chloroform and opened the valve. The chloroform level in the air across the lab started to increase. In less than 2 minutes, he could see people going to a sleep state through live CCTV footage in that room.

They stepped out of the room and reached the collider in the next 5 minutes. They crossed with at least 15-20 sleeping people on the way. The collider was emitting boson particles under a controlled environment.

Dr. Kevin said, "Here you go. You can take as much as you want and leave in the next few minutes before anyone else gets alerted. I hope you have everything required to collect your fuel."

Alien 1 fixed one end of its fibre roll at the end of the collider and started pressing some buttons on the other end of the roll. The fibre started attracting the boson particles in the next few seconds, and Kevin could see a colour change in the fibre roll. He was surprised at the technological advancement of their neighbours while humans were just at the beginning of this invention.

He dreamed of getting the technology from the aliens and introducing it to Earth. That would be the biggest revolution in human evolution, like the invention of fire. He wanted to set his name in human history, and he knew well that this would be his best bet. So, he made up this plan with the aliens and decided to make this mutual agreement to get their prototype for the energy generator.

The aliens took what they needed, and all three of them came out of the collider lab and moved back to the lawn where the aliens had landed their plane. Doctor was excited to get the prototype from the aliens, and he was so proud to complete the mission without any bloodshed. Alien 2 went inside their plane and came back with a prototype. The prototype was hand-sized, and they said the engines in that prototype could generate enough power to run the plane for many light years. Doctor was jaw-dropped, looking at the small engine. While he was examining the model in his hands, they met some flashy lights. The aliens were clearly not comfortable with those lights.

Sandy and Sara came out with their mobile cameras and were continuously clicking photos of the doctor with the aliens. They had their respiratory masks on, which they must have got from the secret chamber in the basement.

Frustrated by the flashlights, the aliens said, "Doctor, ask them to stop those lights. Else they will be destroyed in no time."

"Sandy, hold on. Stop clicking photos. Please, listen to me," Doctor appealed to him to stop.

"Doctor, we just heard the announcement on the radio. They said we will be rewarded with more money if we report this UFO. Why should I let it go, doctor? Also, surprisingly, we got to know about you as well now. You are a betrayer, doctor."

"Hold on, Sandy. You still don't understand the situation here. I have done this for the betterment of the entire human race. Better turn off the video recording. I will explain everything to you later. They must leave now."

"Sorry, doctor. You have dozed off everyone here. I can't leave you all just like that," Sandy said, speaking with his camera recording on with flash.

The next moment, Alien1 triggered its IR Laser gun, and Sandy vanished.

Alien1 spoke with a fake gratitude, "He must have been mixed with matter now. Sorry, we can't tolerate this light beam for long, as our skin could burn on this light frequency. So, I can't help the situation."

Sara, who was standing speechless so far, raised her gun at once towards the doctor. "You cheat, betrayer. You are not supposed to be alive, and you have put us all at risk. Get lost."

The doctor fell in bloodshed, and the prototype he had in his hand fell. He uttered, "You made a mistake, Sara. You pushed the entire human race centuries back."

She didn't give a thought to him anymore and shifted her aim towards the aliens. But she was not quick enough to win the situation.

The next laser beam from the aliens' gun killed her in seconds, and she disappeared into a stream of atoms in the next few seconds.

Doctor, dying, asked the aliens for help. "Please help me. I helped you get whatever you wanted, and please help me to survive."

"Sorry, doctor. We don't want our cover blown. We are supposed to keep stealth across this galaxy ride and are not able to help you now," Alien1 leaned down and took back the prototype.

Doctor uttered his last words, "God particles."

The orphaned radio at the gate gave the announcement to nobody: "UFO that we saw some time back crossed our station again.

*****

The Alchemist's Dream

It is tough to find such a calm place in the heart of the city. It is none other than Dr. John's laboratory. It is his house as well. He stays there all the time to finish and wrap up the final stage of his project. His assistant, Ryan, also stays there with him.

The doctor resumed the research at 8 a.m., even before Ryan woke up. He looked excited to welcome the results of his few years of research. Things were scattered in his room. He had no time to arrange them. Ryan entered the room with a pinch of a yawn.

"Come on, Ryan. You are too late today. Do you know what happened last night after you slept?"

"What happened, Doctor? How many days should I stay awake waiting for better work from you? I couldn't control my sleep last night after finishing house chores. What happened?" asked Ryan, his eyes half open.

He was surprised looking at the new green solution filled in big jars in front of him.

"This is the X-factor solution I found last night, Ryan. I cracked the hidden codes and found the matter of life in the form of this solution. I think, by mixing this, I can complete my stem cell research and create humans myself."

"I don't understand anything, Doctor," replied Ryan, hands on his head.

"I will simplify this for you. How does an embryo turn into a human?"

"Through mitosis and meiosis. Cells split into tissues, and tissues into organs. Simple as that," replied Ryan.

"Exactly. But how does an embryo know the final human form it should complete with?"

"They must have some messages through DNA strands. DNA gives the design, and other cells build the body. Am I right, Doctor?" asked Ryan.

"Good boy. You know up to this level. Do you know what the human body is made of?"

"Bones, muscles, fat, cholesterol, etc., Doctor," replied Ryan.

"But my answer to the same question would be different, Ryan. The human body is completely made of modified forms of oxygen, hydrogen, carbon, nitrogen, etc., along with some more natural elements."

"So, how do you make a man with all these things?"

"An embryo contains all the design messages within stem cells. So, all these years, I was struggling to find the energy within these stem cells that makes them grow into a proper human. Last night, I managed to solve that missing X-factor. When placed inside this liquid, a stem cell can easily turn into a proper human. I can convert a normal cell into a stem cell and make it grow into a human within the next few hours. I will be a god then," said the doctor, closing his eyes and dreaming of his success. Ryan was yawning nearby.

"Ryan, let us get into action. Go and buy the items I have mentioned from the nearby store. We need to start our experiment in the next few hours."

Ryan went to chemical stores to buy all the minerals and raw materials that the doctor suggested.

While Ryan was out buying the ingredients, the doctor took his blood sample and was converting it into a stem cell by adding automatic tissue growth messages. It had information like 65% oxygen, 10% hydrogen coded to that. He was altering existing DNA strands to build tissues automatically using the available raw materials.

By the time the stem cells were ready, the ingredients arrived. They had two cylinders of oxygen, one cylinder of hydrogen, a little nitrogen, and a few packs of other materials like sulphur, chlorine, etc. John already had a big chamber to prepare humans, and all his earlier attempts had failed. He added some preservatives and a pale blue liquid to the tall chamber. The chamber had provisions to connect with all cylinders from the sides. He attached all cylinders to the chamber using side knobs.

"Doctor, what are you going to do?" Ryan looked a little scattered.

"I am going to place my stem cell within this chamber, Ryan. It will then be ready to undergo human evolution from a single cell. This solution I have prepared and added to this chamber is like what it is inside a womb. So, seeding my stem cell in this liquid should grow another Doctor John in the next few hours. All I need to do is add the other ingredients in the right ratio. They should be added through the holes on top of the beaker, and only the right amount must be added. Then my solution will start assembling these nutrients into a new human." The doctor started to dream while explaining the process, and Ryan was yawning from the other side. In his mind, he was cursing the doctor for his stupid experiments.

'How can a small cell placed in a water-like solution turn into a human when a few cylinders are connected? This man has completely gone mad,' Ryan brooded from the corner, but he couldn't be loud just to secure his job. His phone showed five notifications from his girlfriend.

He started releasing oxygen into the chamber. "Ryan, you slowly release hydrogen from the other side. Both should be added at the same time." Doctor and Ryan started the process sincerely.

Ryan was distracted again by a long vibration from his phone. He picked his phone slightly out of his pocket and saw almost six missed calls from his girlfriend, Ananya. Their relationship was already on the brink as he wasn't spending enough time with her. But he couldn't explain his situation where he was stuck with a mad scientist who was driving him crazy. The doctor was strict within the lab and never liked Ryan using his phone inside. So, he kept the phone in his pocket again before the doctor could notice.

As they kept adding magnesium, his phone murmured again. He stood on the other side of the doctor and started replying to Ananya over text while following the doctor's instructions.

Once the gases were added to the chamber in the necessary amounts, the doctor took his notes and started reading the next set of elements to add. As he kept reading, Ryan added them one by one from another opening in the chamber.

"Add 25g of magnesium over that lid, Ryan. Add a pinch of calcium for now. We can add the rest of the calcium once bones start forming. Ryan, quickly add some phosphorus; we need that in DNA formation."

"Doctor, shall I add this full pack of phosphorus?" While asking the doctor about the phosphorus, his love chemistry seemed to have worked out. He managed to console Ananya successfully and got kisses from her in the next message.

"No, just add a small teaspoon quantity for now. I will tell you when to add more," he said while looking at the next set of elements. "Ryan, have you added zinc?"

"Yes, Doctor. All set."

"Let's wait for a few minutes. Just start and increase the oxygen inflow again." He sat on the floor looking at the chamber, anxious like a mom waiting for her delivery moments.

Ryan increased the oxygen inflow and went outside to continue texting Ananya. Suddenly, he heard the doctor shouting from the chamber room. "Ryan! Ryan!" in glee. Ryan came inside the chamber room and was shocked to the core. He could see the formation of a leg-like structure. He was seeing the creation of a new man in front of his eyes, just like a 3D printer. Tissues started to form, and he could see traces of white bones near the foot. It seemed Doctor's replica was on its way.

While everything started well, suddenly they saw a mild spark in the chamber. It quickly turned into a big flame within seconds. They almost had no time to react. The fire moved from the chamber and quickly turned into an electrical fire. Within minutes, the fire spread to half of the room. The doctor started to collect at least his research papers. Ryan initially tried to fight the fire with extinguishers, but it didn't work. They both ran outside to save their lives. By that time, the fire had consumed almost half of the room. The doctor looked shellshocked, never expecting such a fire in his research. They came out of the chamber room and disconnected the power supply at once to avoid the worst.

Firefighters arrived on the scene, and it took them almost an hour to extinguish the fire completely. The police were on the spot and started their investigation. The doctor was deeply saddened by the disastrous end to his research. While watching the remnants of the chamber room from outside, he remembered the half-formed legs.

'So, my research was going in the right direction. Where did I go wrong? Did my stem cell lead to spontaneous human combustion? Do I need to start from zero again? Are all the research papers I have done so far, a waste? Can these lead to another combustion in the future?' Thousands of questions were running through his mind. He felt like something went wrong with his formula and started going through his 1000-page research paper. He was deep in thought.

Once the situation was under control, Ryan tried to reach Ananya again. While trying to pick his phone from his pocket, he felt the empty phosphorus pack. Again, the doctor's voice lingered in his mind, 'No, just add a small teaspoon quantity for now.' He understood what had happened. He stayed quiet to save himself from the situation and crime. While he felt guilty inside, the doctor continued the conversation with him.

"Ryan, no matter how many years it takes, I am not going to give up on this research. I have decided to shred these papers and start fresh. I will need your support, Ryan." While the doctor patted him on the back, Ryan threw the empty phosphorus pack out the window.

*****

Rivalry

"Doctor, how is Ananya now? What happened to her?" Ananya's father, Aaditya, was drenched in sweat, tense, and staring at the doctor's face, desperate to hear anything.

"Ananya is poisoned. It looks like a murder attempt to me. She has been given poison. I don't know how possible it is to save her. We are fighting hard from our side, but... this could turn into a police investigation. Does she have any enemies? Because we haven't seen such a strong poison dosage before. Check if she has any other problems as well," the doctor concluded, rubbing his sharp nose doubtfully.

Aaditya left AMS Hospital with a clouded mind. He was struggling to connect the dots. He decided to delve into her case himself. He started dialling all her friends to understand what might have gone wrong.

After checking with a few of her friends, he got his first clue from her friend Rajesh.

"Uncle, Ananya is so sweet and definitely couldn't have made such hard enemies that quickly, but..." Rajesh was stammering.

"Come on, Rajesh... I don't have much time. Any clue you can give me now is priceless."

"Uncle, Ananya was in a relationship with a boy called Joseph."

"Was or is?"

"Joseph is no more, uncle. He was killed a few days back. And she was furious after finding out what happened to Joseph. I think his murder might be linked to Ananya's poisoning."

"But Rajesh... how do you conclude that it was murder?"

"I was there, uncle. I was with him. It was a cold-blooded murder. Last week, at midnight, we tried to enter that corner house. He went inside ahead of us. Within minutes, we heard bashing and slapping sounds. He was lying in a pool of blood. He was badly beaten to death."

"So, Ananya could have tried to take revenge for Joseph's death?"

"Possibly, uncle. She was already fuming with revenge and waiting for her chance."

Rajesh provided a firm lead for Aaditya. Thanking him hurriedly, Aaditya rushed back home.

He started searching Ananya's room. Joseph had a gorgeous smile in the photos hidden under her pillow. He found a few more pictures of Joseph: dark complexion, sharp nose, and a handsome hunk. No wonder Ananya fell for him. He continued searching in her room. There it was... a vial labelled 'Plasmodium samples' next to her bed. He almost understood her plan now.

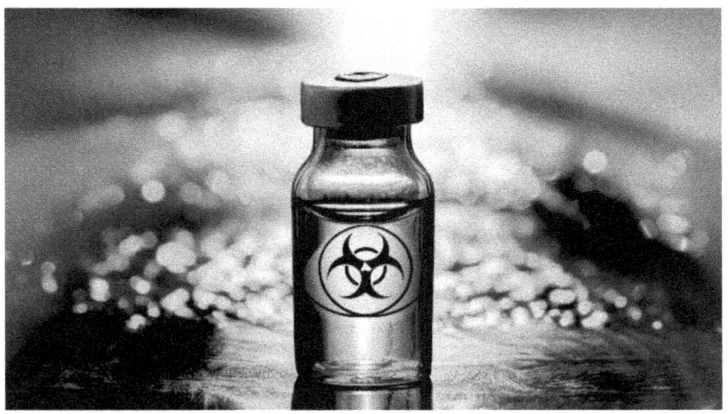

"She must have used these samples to take revenge. But who could have poisoned her?" He couldn't solve the mystery completely.

He decided to visit the corner house to find more answers. It was late at night, and there were no lights in the house. As he got closer to the entrance window, he heard the voices of two police constables. He approached them quietly and started listening to their conversation.

"Man, what a moment it was. Almost six months of searching to catch him. Our inspector banged on the door, and that guy was standing as still as wood. For a moment, he didn't even know what to do next. We all rushed to catch him, and he had that pill in his shirt collar. I went to hold his hand at once, but I was a fraction of a second too late. He placed the pill in his mouth."

"Gosh! What happened then?"

"Nothing... we couldn't save him. He died on the spot from the strong poison. All our six months of effort went in vain," the constable explained with great anguish.

Aaditya felt a mild pat from behind. It was Rajesh. He sighed, "Shhh!" and took Aaditya out of that room. Rajesh urged him to return to MMS Hospital to see Ananya in her final moments.

Aaditya rushed back to Mosquito Multi Specialty Hospital. Ananya was on her deathbed. The doctor came out inconclusively and said, "Sorry, Aaditya, we tried our best to save Ananya. But this seems to be a new type of poison named cyanide, and we don't have an antidote for it. This is completely new to our Anopheles species.

Sorry again. You can go in and meet Ananya one last time." The doctor hurried out of the ward.

He went inside to meet his little daughter.

"Dad... please forgive me... I was completely blinded by vengeance and lost my battle...!" Her wings stopped for the last time...

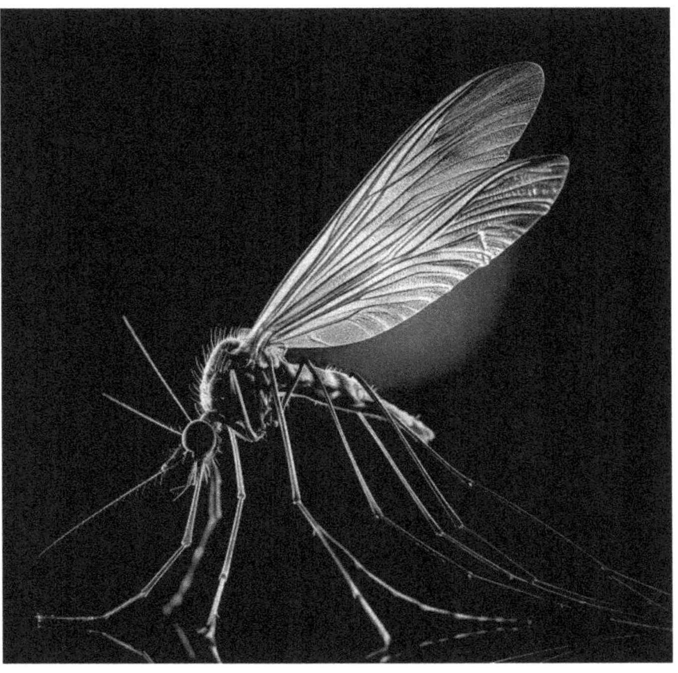

*****

The Masked Hearts

Wednesday morning didn't start well. My mind was clouded with the recent conflicts with Tarika, and I couldn't focus. Conflicts with Tarika over the last two nights have left me feeling confused. I needed to settle things down to focus on other matters. I logged into my laptop with all these thoughts weighing on me.

For a moment, I was taken aback by the sweet surprise of my promotion. I have been promoted to the General Manager level. This was completely unexpected, and I understood that it was given to me by my boss for my dedication and hard work over the last six months. I jumped to the salary section. It was a good hike, but the price I have paid for this role was Tarika's distress. The last six months have been a rollercoaster in my project, and I was not able to spend much time with Tarika, which has already put her under stress. And obviously, it has carried over to me nowadays.

"Tarika joined my project almost a couple of years ago when I was leading the team. Since we both worked together in the same team, we had ample time to spend together every day as friends. Over time, our friendship blossomed into love. As one of the top performers, she was always dear to me and my confidante in the team. Now, our love is over a year old. It took us a year to transition from friendship to love. We shared stories from kindergarten to college, from breakfast to supper, and soon realized we were meant to share our lives together. However, things changed over the last few months. I was moved to another team to stabilize their deliverables and had to leave Tarika's team. It was our first separation in our love life, and I could not spend as much time with her as before. Our time together dwindled, and the distance grew. Still, I managed to call her at bedtime and make her sleep. But things worsened over the last couple of months.

New team, new challenges, new people—I had to spend round the clock on my new project. I even had to shift my lunch timings and coffee breaks to align with my new crew. Despite seeing my struggle firsthand, she began to distance herself from me over time. Even skipping a good morning or good night message led to complaints from her, as if I didn't care anymore. I tried to make amends and please her whenever possible, but now this promotion email is giving me mixed feelings.

I went straight to her desk and asked for a private chat for a few minutes. She came out to the lobby looking puzzled, as it had been days since I spoke to her like this. I was filled with mixed emotions, knowing this could add to my burdens and push her further away.

She started, "Mmmm. Tell me Krish."

I continued, "What happened Tarika? Are you still angry with me?"

"Nothing of that sort. Tell me, Krish," she replied with a slight grin.

"Tari, I got a promotion email this morning. I am now promoted to the General Manager level."

Her mood completely shifted, and she became happy for me. She was all smiles and congratulated me.

"I knew you would get better rewards for your hard work. You deserve this, da. I am so happy for you," she said, genuinely pleased.

"Thanks, da. All my success is because of you and my family. I will always be grateful to you," Krish said, squeezing her hands tightly to show his warmth.

We forgot about our previous night's rift and had our usual couple conversation. After discussing various topics, we circled back to time management. She began hesitantly,

"Krish, you were already busy before. Now with this new role, you might forget about me completely."

"Not at all, Tari. How could I forget you? It's just that I haven't found time to talk to you, but you're always on my mind."

"But how would I know that? I think about you all the time. But we also need time to share with each other, right?"

"Absolutely. Let me plan, Tari. Shall we plan for a movie on Friday?"

"When? I am always ready to come out with you. It is all about your availability. You need to make your plans," she said, longing to spend some time with me.

"I will confirm with you sometime, Tari. I will distribute my work to peers, book tickets, and confirm with you."

Again, I checked for any movie availability for Friday evening and saw the 'Saathiya' movie re-release. I pinged her on IM.

"Tari, are you okay with the 'Saathiya' movie? It is a re-release, but I would love to watch it with you again."

"Sure, I am fine with any movie with you. All I need is popcorn and cold coffee. Order that as well," she replied.

I booked two tickets to "Saathiya" and sent her the tickets over WhatsApp. I could sense rejuvenation in her messages. I wanted to give her some quality time and outings.

Friday Afternoon:

I met her before lunch. She was as gorgeous as ever, well-groomed for her outing with me. It reminded me of our early days when she used to come in stunning attire regularly. After we committed, she toned down to casual attire. Today, she seemed revived. She seems to be taking steps to keep us close. I went for lunch with my friends and returned to my desk.

I planned and finished almost all my tasks for the day to keep me free for the evening. Just as I was about to wrap up, my boss dropped a bomb on my plan.

He came anxiously towards my cubicle and started without waiting for my greeting.

"Hi Krish, I badly need your help. Varun, who was preparing our monthly report, had to leave early due to a personal emergency. You need to finish the report and send it to the onshore team by the end of the day. You may need some inputs from the onshore team. Have a call with them and coordinate once. Sorry for this last-minute task, Krish. But I couldn't rely on anyone else who could finish the report flawlessly on the first attempt. That's why I am fully relying on you now. Hope it is fine for you?"

I felt like a cornered mouse and couldn't say anything else but nod my head. More than the report, I was stressed about how to handle Tari now. Once my manager left, I pinged Tari and asked her to come to my desk. I knew it was going to wreak havoc, but I decided to manage whatever came my way. I couldn't break my boss's trust.

She came to my cubicle, sat next to me, and started playing with a Rubik's cube on my desk. Playing sincerely, she asked, "When shall we start, Krish?"

"Tari... It looks like I may get delayed. I got some unexpected tasks at the last minute. I couldn't say no as others had to leave."

I saw her face change. Like a flower blooming and withering in a day, her face turned red with anger and then pale with disappointment within a minute. She didn't say a word. That scared me even more. She stood up and tried to leave. I held her hand.

"Tari, please say something. Don't go without saying anything. I know I am bad at managing this. But please, my situation needs me now."

All this while, she was looking down. When I asked her to speak, she looked at me straight. I couldn't face her. Her eyes were in tears, expressing her anger.

"Thanks, Krish, for teaching me another lesson, not to expect anything from you. Did I ask you for a movie night? You made the plan and now you've cancelled it. What is my role in this? Why should I even feel hurt? I don't know, Krish. But better leave me alone for some time. Marry your career, Krish. Please don't call me anywhere outside. This will be the last outing I plan with you. You don't need to take the pain of calling me again."

Tari walked away, fully broken. But I couldn't help her fully. I waited for the situation to calm down. After she left my desk, I resumed my work without any interest. I was almost fully dependent on the onshore team for the report input. Ironically, I had to send the same report back to the onshore team. Basically, I was just doing their documentation work. When it was almost 4:30 p.m., I joined the call with my onshore team.

"Hi Krish, how are you?" - That was Mike on the other end.

"I am good, Mike. How are you? How are things going?"

"All good, Krish. So, it is Friday evening. What are your plans?"

I was furious and helpless at the same time. That felt like rubbing salt on my wound.

"Not bad, Mike. How about yours?"

"Good, Krish. Thanks. Listen, I have some important updates for you. Since it is almost year-end and the weekend, the onshore team is planning to go for a team outing and dinner. So, we may need to cancel this call."

"But Mike, how can I finish this report without your inputs?"

"Well, we have got a day waiver from customers, and we can send this to customers on Monday. So, you don't need to work on this today, Krish."

I was just punching the air on the other side of the call. I was full of smiles and felt relieved. I thanked him and without waiting a second, went and updated my boss. He was happy and relieved too. I didn't expect this sudden shift in momentum. But it happened.

I ran straight to Tarika's cubicle. Almost everyone from her team had left, and she was just sitting there for no reason. She was totally angry at me. She was acting like she had some busy work. She didn't care to face me. I went and pulled her chair.

"Tari, look at me. We can still go to movie. I just got my task moved to Monday."

She stared at me, full of disbelief.

"Tari, I'm sorry. I know it was my mistake. I should have prioritized us over work."

Still no reply from her. This silence slightly provoked my ego. I had expected her to accept my apology right away. Her silence stoked my ego.

"Tari, please listen. You are more important to me than anyone else."

"You should have said that when I walked away from your desk in tears, Krish."

"But I wanted to show you through actions, not just words, Tari."

"So, what have you done now, Krish?"

"I talked to my team and cancelled my meeting. I also requested an extra day to finish the report. I've freed up my schedule for today."

"Thank you, Krish. But I'm not in the mood to go out anymore. I'm planning to go home soon."

"Tari, these fights are temporary. I know you're angry, but don't let our good moments be wasted in this anger. You can show me this anger even while we're watching a movie or having dinner. Come on, Tari."

Tarika was slowly entering my zone. I had finally sown some confusion in her.

"Don't try to convince me, Krish. I know you'll somehow try to persuade me and take me out. But I want to stay stubborn today."

"You know what will happen, Tari. Please. We don't have much time. It's almost 5 p.m. If we start now, we can finish the movie and dinner and go home happily. Why choose anger over happiness? Tari, just think for a minute and come, please. I'll wait outside for you."

Relief washed over me. It felt like old times, and I felt happy and relieved. I knew we still had challenges ahead, but for now, I was grateful. I walked out and began waiting for her. I knew she could make me wait, but she never made me wait anytime. She came out in a couple of minutes.

"Don't be happy that I came for you. I came for myself. I dressed up for today's outing, and I didn't want to waste that. I came just for myself, Krish," Tarika said, adjusting her makeup. I simply enjoyed seeing her expressions. I saw her face turning bright again. Like a kid getting a chocolate bar, she started smiling with tears.

The rest of the day was truly memorable. We nearly finished two buckets of popcorn and sang 'Saathiya' together. She rested her head on my shoulder and held my hand tightly during the climax. I felt her tears on my shirt as the movie neared its end. We had dinner and then went bowling. The tightness of her hug meant a lot to me. Later, we went to a nearby restaurant for her favourite kebabs and falooda. Our day ended with more bowling and her energetic dance after scoring a strike. We laughed a lot that day, and the earlier fight made the moments even more special. It turned out to be a memorable day. But despite all the enjoyment, one thing weighed on my mind throughout the day.

It was a lie I told her to convince her. Although the meeting was cancelled by the onshore team, I used the situation to my advantage. I lied to her that I cancelled my appointments and came for her. I didn't intend to, but I felt compelled to pacify her. It was one of the few lies I've ever told her, and I'm certain it was only to make her happy, not to deceive her in any way. The lie was necessary to restore some peace. But someday, when I feel things are better, I will confess to her.

"Tari, I hope someday you'll find some solace in this lie and understand my intentions. I believe a lie to make someone smile is better than a truth that hurts someone. Still, a lie is a lie, and I owe you an apology."

Tarika's Diary

Morning blues continued with my grumpy boss's call on the way to the office. I reached my desk, logged into my laptop, and opened my first email. I started reading through the minutes of the meeting email sent by my boss. But my thoughts lingered on Krish. I couldn't focus, and started thinking of how we were a few months back.

We both worked together on the same project for a long time. He used to share everything with me, and so did I. He was an amazing leader, always listening to and respecting others' opinions. I liked his charming nature and his way of working with people. I had seen him solving many issues with ease, and I started developing a deep respect for him. It was just a matter of time before my respect turned into love.

Almost a year back, we confessed our love for each other. We had a beautiful year together, and it was almost like a dream come true. I saw his dedication and his genuine care for people. He was always there for me. We both used to go out every weekend and sometimes during weekdays as well. He used to be the one planning everything meticulously. He used to share all his stories, and we used to laugh together.

But the last few months were different. He got moved to a different project, and we couldn't spend much time together. Though I saw his struggle, I missed his presence. I missed his calls and messages. Initially, I thought it was just a phase and things would be back to normal soon. But it didn't. I felt isolated and started getting frustrated. I started complaining about every little thing. I knew it wasn't helping either of us, but I couldn't stop myself.

I was lost in my thoughts when I felt a hand on my shoulder. It was Krish.

He came to my desk before lunch and reminded me about our evening plans. I was so excited for our outing tonight.

After a long time, I took extra care with my grooming. I wore his favourite black top, a birthday gift from him. I had yearned to escape my hectic schedule for a day and spend a complete evening with Krish. However, he delivered a mini heartbreak in the evening when he said we needed to postpone our plans. I was utterly shattered; my excitement drained away within minutes. Yet, I believe that disappointment paved the way for us to thoroughly enjoy today. It was like a movie with a disappointing trailer and low expectations, but it ended up being deeply satisfying to the core.

The movie 'Saathiya' will always hold a special place in my heart. During every small fight between the lead pair, I saw reflections of Krish and myself on screen. I cried my heart out, nestled on his shoulder, cherishing those moments deep within. Some moments are too precious to write down in this diary. Later, we went to a restaurant and enjoyed our favourite dishes. Bowling has never been my forte, especially snow bowling; I had never scored a strike before. But today, something clicked inside me, and I managed to knock down several strikes. We danced on cloud nine. What a beautiful day it was.

But...

But...

But...

But there was one thing that kept bothering me. I didn't expect that lie from Krish. I enjoyed the day with a pinch of salt. Although he's good at convincing me, I couldn't understand why he chose to lie this time. When he went to the restroom and asked me to pay at the restaurant using his mobile, I accidentally touched an email notification and ended up on his Outlook, wanting to reread his promotion email.

I noticed a meeting cancellation notification sent that evening. When I opened it, the reason was it was an 'Onshore Dinner Party'. So, the meeting was originally cancelled due to a party and had nothing to do with our day out. Yet, he decided to cover it up. It wasn't a big deal, but I felt a bit disappointed knowing he hadn't done it for me. I was initially happy that he tried for me and spent time with me, but learning it was pure coincidence left me disappointed.

I decided not to guilt-trip him and chose not to confront him about it. It wouldn't be healthy for our relationship. However, I do expect him to be truthful in the future. I'll wait to see how long he keeps this from me. I'll wait for him to come clean someday, without bringing it up myself. I won't show that I'm aware of this incident and will let him resolve it on his own. I'm uncertain how I'll react when that day comes. I may take it lightly or question his intentions, but I simply hope for honesty.

Someday, if he reads my diary, perhaps he'll understand my feelings. I no longer harbour anger toward him, just some disappointment.

Yes, we have our disagreements, but it's better to understand him, not to hurt him.

Yes, we argue at times, but it's to seek your attention and time, not to hurt you.

With love

Tarika.

*****

Nyra's Secret Gift

"This is the best opportunity for you to speak to her. Don't miss this chance, dude. Also, express your love to her. She'll be in a good mood and will accept your proposal," Helix urged Nexus for the thousandth time.

"I know, Helix. But I'm a little scared and hesitant to open to Nyra. I think it would be better to start my proposal by gifting her something she likes. It needs to be something she could fall for and be impressed with at first sight."

"When did you start loving her, Nexus? At least two years ago? I've never seen anyone wait so long, especially in this era."

"You're half right. It's been almost four years since I started admiring her. I first saw Nyra at a robot fair where she was a lead coordinator. I fell for her at first sight, and from then on, there was no turning back. All I haven't done is speak my heart out to her."

"How are you going to impress her then? Time is running out. You need to propose to her this year. I can help you as much as I can, Nexus."

"Well, I need to think about what I can give her. This first gift should be the best gift she's ever received. She loves pets and has many at home. But what doesn't she have?" He entered deep thought. Suddenly, an idea flashed in his mind. He snapped his fingers and got up happily, a risky idea forming in his mind.

Snapping his fingers, he said, "She had a pet a few months ago that died of sickness. Getting her a similar pet could be the best gift I could give. She might love it."

"That sounds great, Nexus. So, what are you waiting for? Let's start searching for the pet today itself. What is the name of that pet species?"

"Here's the catch, dude. I don't know the species name. This species is almost extinct, and the government has prohibited harming or keeping it domestically. If we still try to get a pet from that species, it needs to be top secret."

"Do you have any photos of that pet? We can use them as a reference to find the species in the market."

He pulled out an old photo from his phone and showed it to Helix. Nyra was a stunning beauty, glossy and perfect in her creation. In the photo, she was holding the pet to the side. Nexus pointed at it and said, "Check this out, Helix. This is the pet I've been talking about. She loved this pet but couldn't keep it for long."

"This species looks familiar, Nexus, but I can't figure out where I've seen it. We can check nearby pet outlets."

They both raced to nearby pet outlets and showed the photo of the pet to the store attendants.

"Sir, do you have any pets like this one in the picture? We're looking for baby pets and are willing to pay any price."

The store attendants were taken aback upon seeing the photo. They asked Helix to come aside.

"Sir, these species are almost extinct, and the government doesn't encourage selling them anymore."

"Oops. So, what we were looking for is illegal, isn't it?"

"Yes, sir. But we can help you through the black market. We have some options there. Would you like to try?"

After a deep thought, Helix and Nexus decided to go ahead with the pet sellers. The store attendant closed the front door and led them through a secret passage. The passage ended with a bright light beneath their feet. They realized they were walking on a glass floor. Below, they saw glass cubicles having extinct species of animals. They walked across the huge hall, searching for the species they were looking for.

They couldn't find the species they were looking for. They almost went through the hall twice, but the one they were seeking was missing. The store attendant realized something was wrong. He went to a chamber at the end of the room and discovered the species had escaped. They saw small potholes at the end of the room through which the species could have escaped.

"Sir, something seems wrong here. The species must have escaped. I need to alert my guards and search the surroundings."

"Is there any way to get them back?"

"Hopefully, sir. We are more powerful than them. They won't be able to escape us for long. We should have them back soon," the store attendant pointed at the empty chamber.

"Alright. We'll take our leave now."

Both Nexus and Helix left the shop. They continued their search for the next few days but couldn't find the species anywhere. Nexus almost gave up. Helix kept trying from his side.

Nyra's birthday approached, and Nexus decided to wish her empty-handed. On the way to Nyra's place, he stopped to recharge. He felt something strange around him. There was a slight disturbance behind the bushes and trees where he was resting. Without making a noise, he went to check. No one was there. But he suspected something beneath his feet. He saw a lid beneath his feet and decided to check inside.

He slowly entered the lid in stealth mode and walked down the dark passage. There he saw something interesting. The thing he had been searching for all these days was resting there. The species were sleeping as a clan in hiding. They looked panicked by the external world and didn't want to face it. They were living in isolation. They didn't notice Nexus entering their habitat. They were in a deep sleep. There was a beautiful tiny baby of the species sleeping next to its mother. Initially, Nexus was hesitant to approach them. He felt pity for them as they were the last few of their species. After a moment of thinking, he decided to take a baby from the group. He had a bag of flowers for Nyra. He took the baby and placed it in the flower bag. It was sleeping from exhaustion. Before the others woke up, Nexus left the same way. He was thrilled to find the one he had been searching for over the past ten days.

Just two more hours until Nyra's birthday, and it would be perfect timing if he started now. He accelerated toward her house and arrived on time. She was upstairs. He climbed up the back stairs without making a noise. She was already looking out the window.

His clock showed 12 a.m., and the date changed to 7/13/3168. He surprised her from behind. She was shell-shocked and happy to see him suddenly there. Before uttering a word, they hugged each other. They knew what they were up to.

"Happy Birthday, Nyra."

"Thanks, Nexus. I didn't expect you here. How did you manage to hack my security?"

"I'm not new to this place, right? I know this place as well as I know you, Nyra."

"Is that so? What else do you know about me?"

"You might understand better when you see my gift. A memorable gift for you, Nyra."

Nexus handed over his gifts to Nyra.

She opened his digital letter using her encryption keys. It was one of the best love letters of the 31st century. It ended like this:

"To my wonderful Nyra (59.78.234.566.345)

When the whole world runs out of silicon, I will burn mine and give you my silicon ashes. When the whole world runs out of electricity, I will give you my last drop of electrons. When the whole world runs out of robots, I will be the last one to die before you.

I will stay with you forever. Can we become partners to lead our lives together?

I wish to merge my subnet with your subnet.

With lots of love,

Nexus (116.57.84.23.476)

Nyra couldn't control her mercury tears and shed a few drops. She looked completely impressed. Nexus gave her his other gift as well: a flower bag with the baby species on top. She couldn't hold her joy upon seeing it.

*****

About The Author

Praveenkarthik K has around 15 years of experience in Software Engineering. As part of his assignments, he was deputed to London for four years, during which he gained global exposure both professionally and personally. He began his journey as a software developer and is currently serving as a project manager with a leading consultancy firm.

Praveen developed a habit of reading at the age of six through comics and transitioned into authorship with his first Tamil book, Kadavul Thugalgal, at the age of 32. Drawing inspiration from renowned Tamil author Sujatha, he aims to prove himself as a versatile writer across various genres. He has written and published three Tamil books as eBooks on Kindle. Praveen's writing journey has earned him some of the best accolades of his life for his versatility. He loves to write science fiction and romance dramas, which naturally led to his first book, Octales.

Beyond his writing endeavours, Praveen is a Tech YouTuber (Channel name – Prakavids) with 500+ subscribers. He is also a long-distance runner with aspirations to complete full marathons soon. He has a deep passion for music, quilling crafts, photography, yoga, and is a jack of these trades.

He currently resides in Chennai, India, with his wife Kavitha and their child Mikhal. When he's not engaged in any of the above interests, Praveen enjoys movies and music.

His latest book, Octales, is his first English book and his most challenging venture to date. Some stories in this collection were written 10 years ago, brewed over time to finally get published.

You can reach Praveen on Twitter @paverik1988 or visit his website at https://blog458897615.wordpress.com/ for more writings.

*****